**Merlin Tyana**
Book two
***Mirrors***

Merlin Tyana, a mysterious figure who appears always during a storm, finds some more murders to solve or prevent. He always disappears when his work is done.

**Merlin Tyana**
Book two
***Mirrors***
© 2004 - 2011- 2013 by C. D. Moulton
all rights reserved: no part of this publication may be reproduced or transmitted in any form or by any means, either electronic or mechanical, including photocopy, recording, or any other information retrieval system, without permission in writing from the copyright holder/publisher, except in the case of brief quotations embodied in critical articles or reviews.

This is a work of fiction. Any resemblances to persons living or dead is purely coincidental

## Contents

| | | |
|---|---|---|
| Foreword | pg. | 1 |
| Mirrors | pg. | 2 |
| Final Tour | pg. | 16 |
| Pictures | pg. | 28 |
| Well, Well. | pg. | 41 |
| Rest Stop | pg. | 50 |
| But Then... | pg. | 57 |
| Smoke | pg. | 65 |

## About the author

CD Moulton has traveled extensively over much of the world both in the music business, where he was a rock guitarist, songwriter, and arranger, and in an import/export business. He has been everything from a bar owner to auto salvage (junkyard) manager, longshoreman to high steel worker, orchid grower to landscaper, tropical fish farmer to commercial fisherman. He started writing books in 1983 and has published more than 300 books as of January 1, 2020. His most popular books to date are about research with orchids, though much of his science fiction and fantasy work has proven popular. He wrote the CD Grimes, PI series and the Det. Nick Storie series, among other works.

He now resides in Gualaca, Panamá, where he writes the Clint Faraday mystery series, plays music with friends – and pursues his favorite ways to spend his time: beach bum and roaming the mountain jungles doing botanical research. He has lately become involved in fighting for the rights of the indigenous people, who are among he closest friends, and in fighting the extreme corruption in the courts and police in Panamá.

He offers the free e-book, *Fading Paradise*, that explains what he has been through because of the corruption.

CD is the discoverer of the Chadam Prrotocol for curing cancer. Facebook page Ambrosia peruviana for cancer

## Foreword

I wrote a collection of stories based, originally, on the idea of The Mysterious Harley Quinn by Agatha Christie. I combined the names of two of the world's foremost magicians, Apollonius of Tyana, who actually existed and Merlin, who probably didn't.

It didn't take long to stray from the idea. Less than half of the second story.

Merlin Tyana is a mysterious character who appears at critical times, always during a severe thunderstorm and generally when there is a love or life in peril, suggests a solution to the problem – usually involving murder – and disappears.

These stories are written in the "Old English" tradition. I've found that most people over thirty five are sick to death of the graphic sex and violence and lack of plot in the "modern" works. It doesn't connect with today's editors that they can't name the bestseller of two months ago, much less a year ago, yet Agatha Christie, Ngaio Marsh, Rex Stout, et al are still strong sellers long after most of them are dead. If you say "locked room" to mystery fans they say "John Dickson Carr, of course." Poirot, they know Christie. Nero Wolfe, they know Stout.

Whatever. The first collection was very well received and I don't claim to be the writer Christie or the others were, but many people tell me they like my stories and that's what it's about, isn't it?

## *Mirrors*

Lydia LaVerne slipped off the final thin veil, dropped it, stood motionless for two beats, turned to full profile and swayed off the narrow stage to loud catcalls and much appreciative applause.

How she pitied them. Most of them. Pathetic sick losers who paid ridiculous prices to watch her take off her clothes to the beat of a second-rate three piece "band" – that was all drums and stripper clichés on the piano and horn.

Well, it was a living.

Truth be told it was a very good living! She made what a lot of executives made in a week in four six minute dances a night five nights a week. Two hours a week and she made what that CEO following her backstage made in forty hours.

She could stoop to blackmail and clean him out. He had a wife and three teenage kids. Instead she told him he was sweet, but she didn't and wouldn't date a customer – very certainly not a married one.

He whined a bit and she spent a few minutes telling him a woman who would date a married man was a fool or a whore. There was no middle ground and she was neither. If the man were to actually leave his wife for her how long would it be until he left her for another bimbo? He proved by even considering it that he couldn't be trusted.

She cut his reply off and told him to think about it. A man and a woman were alike in that area. If they cheat on one they would cheat on another. It was what they were.

And what she wasn't. Thanks, but no thanks.

He just stood there as she closed the door. Quietly. No slamming. He would be back next show, but would know better than to try that again.

*Mirrors*

He was the type who would send her some much too-expensive gift – that she would refuse, then he'd try something else and she'd tell him the next thing he gave her was going to his wife. She did not accept gifts from married men.

He'd go away. She knew how to handle most types.

She had everything planned for the future. She already had enough saved to go into a business when her looks or her figure started to go.

Well, she had good genes. Her mother was still a head-turner at fifty two and she was the spitting image of her. If she kept the ability to make money like at the present for just ten more years and could save at the same rate as lately she would be a millionaire – even with a yearly trip to see the world.

She was lucky, really, but believed absolutely that luck was not enough in life. One must justify existence in some small manner in all cases and must justify good luck even more. That was the way life was.

She remembered her father. He had given her her values.

"Honey, you're going to be just like your mother," he had warned her. "You'll spend your whole life with people wanting to give you things.

"It's not real. They want to buy you and you'll despise them and they'll soon despise you if you allow that.

"Your mother does things for people. You see how she is. I'm the luckiest man in the world that she chose me over ten million others who had position and money and education.

"We have something that can't be bought or sold. We love each other, and that's what life's all about. We can share.

"Honey, you have to make choices in life and you have to be responsible for what you choose. You have to find approval from only one person for your life to be worthwhile

*Mirrors*

and that person stares directly into your soul from the mirror every morning.

"Don't let the world tell you what's right or wrong. The world doesn't figure into it. You do what's right because you have to answer to the person in the mirror. Never forget that you have no secrets from that person in the mirror."

He had a lot of conversations with her like that. Even when she was still very young he always treated her as an individual. He would hold her and explain about all kinds of things in just enough detail that she would know what he meant.

"The greatest feeling in the world is to know you've never let the person in the mirror down.

"We'll all die, Honey. That's only part of life. When my time comes I think I'll be able to smile at the person in the mirror and say, 'It was good.'

"That person will answer, 'Yes, it was, wasn't it?'

"A person who can do that has lived well."

He knew he was dying of cancer at the time. He had prepared her for his death. She was just at the horrible awkward age of thirteen when he died and was able to help her mother over the grief.

"He didn't mind, Mom, except that he didn't want you to be alone and made me promise to try to get you to find someone new to share your life with."

She hadn't. Wouldn't. No man could compare to her father. Her mother had patted her and said she had no need of anyone else because her father would be waiting patiently for her to come to him.

Her father, mother and even she, to the greatest extent, were atheists, but believed they would all be together again. Somehow. Somewhen.

*Mirrors*

She sighed, smiled into the mirror and went out for the final show of the evening.

Would her father approve of how she made her living?

Yes. Because of how she made her living. So long as it was look and don't touch and no phony come-on. Don't make promises you won't keep.

She was beautiful, but beauty had no value in itself and she wasn't a "bitch" because of it. It was good genes she had nothing to do with. She was comfortable with it because she didn't have to work at it.

She saw the games some of the girls played and the attitude they projected. They had contempt for those men out there.

Lydia didn't. Most of them were just very lonely, unhappy and lost in life. She was sorry for most of them, even that CEO. He was not a happy person. His coming here proved it. He didn't know why or what was missing in his life and he didn't share anything. He bought what he wanted and figured that was the way of things.

He worshiped money.

Lydia saved money because it was a practical matter. If she ever needed it, it was there. It was independence in some ways, but a prison in others. It would allow her to go places and to live in a certain manner.

Truth be told she wouldn't miss it too much if she didn't have it.

Vanessa Leona almost ran into her coming off the stage. "Did you get that crud, Harry Lord, off your case?" she asked sourly. "He's trying to go through the whole cast here. Bloody bastard thinks he can buy anyone!"

"All you have to do is tell him the next expensive gift will be sent on to his wife and he backs off," Lydia replied.

"Hah-ah! Like bloody hell! He can send me all the expen-

*Mirrors*

sive gifts he wants and wifey won't hear a word of it!" she snarled. "You're so sweet and moral! Ask me, you're just another whore like all of us! That virgin act may get you top billing and more money, but you're no different!

"Bitch!"

"I didn't ask you," Lydia pointed out and went on stage.

"Package for Miss Lydia LaVerne," the uniformed parcel delivery service driver announced when Hilary Archer opened the dressing room door.

"From whom?" Lydia asked.

"H. L.," he replied.

"Harry Lord!" Vanessa spat.

"Mark it refused and send it back," Lydia ordered.

"No return address," the man said, staring at Vanessa, who just "happened" to not be wearing anything.

"Just put it by the door," Vanessa ordered. "You can shove it up the bastard's ass when he comes in tonight!"

The man put the package on the table, took a last look and left.

"Why do you always have to be so vulgar?" Hilary demanded of Vanessa. "Let him gawk at you out front after he pays for it!"

"He can see a little piece of what he'd be paying for," Vanessa retorted. "Maybe that way he'll *come* to the show.

"Lyd, I'm sorry for last night. I'm in a mood and can't shake it. I think I'm getting flu or something. I'll have to go to Dr. Caitlin, I guess."

"Caitlin is an abortionist!" Hilary cried. "You don't go to him for *flu*!"

"No kidding?" Vanessa asked.

"Oh. Again?" Hilary asked. "There's a drawer full of pills

*Mirrors*

right there. They don't work if you don't take them!"

"No kidding?" Vanessa asked.

"So. Trying to tag some poor idiot into a big payoff?" Hilary said. "What? Going to trap him into breaking up with a wife and running off with you?"

"Do you even know who the father is?" Lydia asked, changing the subject. Hilary often tended to protect the clients a bit much.

"Oh, yeah!" she snarled. "He'll get the bill! With interest! Compounded hourly!"

After the show Lydia noted the package was missing, but figured Vanessa had taken it. It would be like her.

Well, Harry Lord wasn't there tonight, anyhow. If he said anything she would simply say she didn't get any gift, which would be the truth, and that she would have told the deliveryman to take it back if she did – which she had done. She would point out that everyone in the place went in and out of the only dressing room so someone might have pilfered it if it was left there.

She would suggest he check to see who signed for it. Nobody did. It would bother her, but it really wasn't any fault of hers.

She didn't work Sunday or Monday so didn't know if Lord was at the show or not. Tuesday was hectic because a convention of longshoremen was in town and that always brought in big crowds and big money.

Vanessa didn't mention flu or abortionists so she'd had that done. A new girl, Kari Karson, came in because Hilary quit, supposedly to take a better job in Liverpool. She would be back in a few days. She got a better job somewhere else once a month, it seemed. They never were.

At the end of the show they were in the dressing room

*Mirrors*

coun-ting the money thrown on the stage. Kari was unbelieving it could be nearly so much. Lydia explained that conventions always sent the tips through the roof.

"But I never made a third this much on my best night in Soho!" she cried.

"This is uptown," Vanessa said. "It is a good haul and I'm going to make double this. I'm doing a private party."

"But they told me I couldn't do private parties if I work here!" Kari cried.

"So don't *tell* them about it, stupid!" Vanessa snarled. "My god, didn't you listen to what they said?"

"Oh. They said to ... sorta ... that the *place* doesn't book private parties and *discourages* their girls ... I see," Kari said. "How do you handle when they try to ... you know ... at a private party?"

"Tell them just how much it will cost them," Vanessa replied. "If they go for it you *really* find out how much you can make in a night!

"I'm out of here! Tomorrow!" She left.

"Oh God, no! I didn't know we were expected to be prostitutes," Kari said, worriedly. "I don't think I can do that."

"They don't," Lydia said. "I certainly don't. I think she's the only one who does. Much, anyhow. Hilary would go out now and then."

"Thank god! I just couldn't!" Kari cried. "That one guy was nice and I might, but he's married and I ... just couldn't."

"Married?" Lydia asked.

"Lord Harry, Vanessa called him."

"Oh. I didn't see him. He tries with every girl here," Lydia said. "Tell him to back off or the wife gets the message."

"I'll make enough without ... that. Won't I?"

"I've got more than a hundred grand in the bank and I'm a virgin, so I guess so!" Lydia replied.

"A virgin? A stripper?" Kari asked. "You're not ...? I mean...?"

"A lesbian? No," Lydia answered. "I don't even have silly ideas about morality or anything and think it's perfectly fine if you want sex. I just want the fairytale ideal. I want my perfect mate to be the only one. Ever."

"What if he never comes along?" Kari asked.

"He will." It was a positive statement.

"Miss LaVerne?"

Lydia tried to dress down enough away from work that people wouldn't recognize her, but it didn't always work out. She had dodged into the tea room when the rain started and had gone to the only open table there, which this man came to at the same time.

She got along with everyone. For some reason men didn't push too hard except at the club – and this one was a HUNK plus! Even in that costume – anyone wearing a trench coat and Homburg in this section was probably an actor – he was gorgeous. He had the most amazing eyes. They seemed to glow.

"Guilty as charged," she replied, smiling. "Last table. We can share?"

"Merlin Tyana. Thanks."

"Have you seen the show?" she asked, figuring that was how he recognized her even if she couldn't picture him among that bunch of losers. He removed the hat and showed thick mahogany hair she wanted very much to run her fingers through.

She suddenly thought of her statement about Prince Perfect

*Mirrors*

to Kari and grinned. *This* one – could be!

"No. I don't go to shows. Your picture is on a billboard I see now and then."

"You're an actor?"

He shook his head and laughed. "No. I'm an analyst. Police work, mostly homicide."

"Are there that many murders around here?" she asked.

"No, but the rents are low if you know where to look and it's close enough to everything."

The waitress came and stared moon-eyed at Merlin as she took their order. Other patrons didn't seem to even notice him.

"I can picture you Sherlocking, somehow. Like the forties and fifties movies from the states. Sexy secretary and the D. A. is out to show you up," she said. "You don't chain smoke and drink all the time, do you?"

"I don't smoke and a drink in a social situation suits me just fine," he answered. "I don't have a beautiful secretary and have never met the D. A. or whatever. No car chases and shootouts and no speedboats and private jets. I've never even been in very much of a fistfight since my early teens. Accountants get more excitement, I suppose.

"I like puzzles."

The waitress brought the tea and scones and reluctantly left, never glancing at her, but with the moon-eyes at Merlin.

"What kind of puzzles?" she asked.

"Oh, like the case down in Soho. Serial sort of thing. Jack the Ripper copycat, in a loose sort of way. Prostitutes getting cut up."

"Where does the puzzle come in?" she asked. "That sounds like some nutcase."

"It doesn't fit," Merlin replied. "It was either a very clever killer – and killers seldom are – or it's a woman who wants it to look like a man.

"A few years ago it would have worked. Now we can tell if there has actually been a sexual assault, even with a prostitute who was ... recently busy.

"An analyst sees things the normal cop on the beat would miss, such as the patterns of bruising and DNA evidence. There are all manner of fascinating clues. A woman doesn't leave the same clues a man would."

"Soho? Kari worked in Soho until last night when she got a much better job here," Lydia said nervously.

"More probably running from danger than being the one we're after, but you never know," Merlin replied. "For instance, how tall is she? Weight?"

"She's small, but not petite," Lydia answered. "Why? Do you know the size of the killer?"

"Within bounds. She's fairly tall and strong, a medium pale complexion from the makeup traces, but that covers more than half the women you see – except that it's stage makeup so she's an actress or dancer.

"That lets you off of the suspect list! You don't use enough makeup to leave traces around.

"Don't let on we've found any clues. We don't want to alert anyone."

Lydia nodded.

"Seeing I've already let that cat out, she'll have a lot of money around and will have a number of gifts the victims were relieved of. Expensive jewelry and such.

"Do you know anyone who fits the description so far? Other than twenty five percent of the women dancers and actors in the section?"

"She wouldn't be in this section, would she?" Lydia asked.

*Mirrors*

"I mean, Soho?"

"She dropped two very telling things from here," Merlin replied. "One, we wouldn't have connected, but two is suspicious.

"She shops at Connelly's, which is two blocks from here, but is still the kind of place locals shop and she had at least one meal at Corbett's. A block from there. Where a lot of theater people eat."

"All of us from the club eat there on rehearsal days," Lydia said. "I can think of ... no. Sorry, but ... no.

"How many have been killed and when?"

"Six we know about so far. About one a month or slightly longer. Usually on a Monday night, but not always."

"Oh, god! We're off on Mondays!" Lydia cried. "Would ... would the killer tend to be ... to have an attitude? To steal things? To be a prostitute herself?"

"It's possible, but doubtful. Maybe a prostitute, but not as a major part of anything. Probably more the moderator type, but she could be someone who goes into rages or something. She'll be a very careful type."

"Careful?"

"Everything to a plan."

"Like, maybe ... get pregnant to trap some schnook?" Lydia asked slowly. "Maybe go off if it doesn't work?"

"Hmmm. Could be. Most likely was married or into a very deep relationship with a man and some prostitute broke it up. She would make excuses for a man, but never for a woman."

"I see. Then it's not Vanessa. She'd take up for the woman every time. She has nothing but contempt for men. She never will have any deep relationships. She's too selfish."

"More likely to be a victim than the killer," Merlin agreed. "The killer might strike at anyone who suspected her so

*Mirrors*

watch who you say anything to. You could be right and dead at about the same time. If you know the killer you're automatically in great danger if anything happens that could identify her. If she even suspects you've figured it out you're next!"

"Well, the rain's letting up. I have to go."

He smiled showing his perfect teeth, replaced the Homburg and was suddenly gone. She glanced up almost immediately after. He should have been between her and the door, but wasn't. She didn't see him anywhere in the shop.

She'd seen lots of disappearing acts so didn't think about it. She was wondering about something else.

After a few minutes she headed toward the club and slipped in the alley door and to the dressing room where she went to the "diary" they kept, made a few notes and went to the CID office to ask a Lt. Forbes about the Soho cases.

If she had been ordinary she wouldn't have gotten the time of day, but she knew a few tricks and Don Forbes would do anything in his power to keep her around for a little longer. He did seem actually to care that someone was killing the women he described as "unfortunate" victims.

She suddenly cried out and dropped the note Don handed her:

*Victim (suspected) #7: Gertrude Simms, AKA Vanessa Leona et. al. behind Club Astra. Body discovered early this morning. Only unusual feature was an expensive diamond necklace. Other victims had no jewelry left on the bodies.*

A note stated the necklace seemed to have been placed after death as the clasp had cut into the flesh when snapped closed and there was no bruising or bleeding. A parcel delivery slip in her pocket from "H. L" had no return address, but the necklace was traced to Fenworthy's Jewels and had been purchased by a Harold Lord, who claimed he had bought it as a surprise for his wife and had no idea how Simms gained possession. The receipt had a microscopic trace of blood on it – and there was none in the pocket or in other items inside the pocket. Clearly also placed after death. She had an early pregnancy termination at the Caitlin Clinic three days ago. Possibly act of father?

"Don, I want to show you something," Lydia said. "I call it one coincidence too many and you will know what to do about it.

"I think there won't be anymore murders if I'm right."

"Ah! You know this Lord character and he was the baby's father? Wife was going to find out and she was blackmailing him?"

"She would, but this is what I think...."


"... and Merlin described her too closely so I checked the diary we keep of the shows we do and sure enough! She was away at the time of every one of them!

"Don did a trace and found she was around every time.

"What she did was take the box, call Vanessa for a private party gig and killed her, then tried to make it look like that poor pathetic Lord person killed her.

"Have you found out why she did it yet? Or is she simply a homicidal maniac?"

"Well, Miss LaVerne, she was born Hilary Collins. For awhile she was living with a man named George Archer, but he took up with a prostitute and ended up with AIDS, which she first thought that he might have transmitted to her, but she was lucky on that count," Capt. Robb replied. "She took the name Archer when she went on stage.

"I suppose she was planning to get even with every

prostitute in the London area even though the one who infected Archer probably died before he did.

"Who is this Merlin you spoke of?"

"Merlin Tyana. An analyst. We talked in a tea shop for a few minutes. I've never seen him since – and I very definitely absolutely and positively *hope* to!

"He works with the police, I believe. Do you know him?"

"No. I've heard of him, but we've never met," he replied. "I rather doubt we ever will if what I've heard can be credited. He's a very elusive type.

"Is LaVerne your real name?"

"No. It's Allison Anne Green. My mother is LaVerne Green. My grandmother was Lydia Anderson. I just sort of combined them."

"Lydia Anderson? The torch singer?" Don Forbes asked. "I have a picture signed by her. My grandfather hung around the stage door after her and said she was the most beautiful creature he'd ever seen and that she was very much the gracious lady.

"I see where you got your looks and talent!"

Lydia smiled at him. She noted he was a very attractive sort and had a soft but strong voice much like her father's and hair that reminded her of Merlin's. Golden brown with rich reddish-bronze highlights and his eyes were actually very sexy and he did have a wonderful sense of humor and he cared about people and he didn't judge them ....

## *Final Tour*

"... and then run it into a chord change, up-register," Marlene Able instructed her band. "We go from 'C' to 'D' there, which is much more effective for this kind of thing."

"You start out as a sort of ballad, then go into rock without changing the beat," Kyle Masterson, her continuity manager (and latest lover) agreed. "It's effective. You can take an old cover like that and make it seem almost new, but you'll have to get an okay from Campbell and he's known for holding you up.

"I'll try to make it some kind of afterthought. 'Oh! By the way! Would you object if Mar did *Wrong Again* as a filler if she does a chord change in the follow?' sort of thing."

"Tell him we might do the song and he could get a re-release of it so he'll make a bundle on royalties," Dan Johns, drums and lights choreographer suggested. "Let him think it's one song on a list. He'll see the chance to make more from an old song and jump on it."

"I agree," Mar replied. "If he thinks we might record it he'll even do a cut deal on it because it's one of those things that almost made it once, but the wrong person did it the wrong way."

"*He* did it!" Archie Plummer, guitars, pointed out.

"Like I said, the wrong person, the wrong way," Mar shot back sourly. "He can write a great song, but if he performs it, it's as good as dead!

"If you can get something on paper we can make it a cover and I'll do an album with that theme. *Mistaken Identity* is doing very well onstage. *Bad Choices* is as good for a cover and I wrote that one. *Dark Waters* and *Love Shark* could have been the theme, but they're too limited. Two songs and the theme's overdone. *Disaster City* fits this one and can be the heavy metal number and I can do a shortened acoustic tearjerker like *Delilah Deception* to fill it out. It's a dark theme, but they're popular now.

"I'll do that one and maybe one more, then I'm going to retire. We can record a couple dozen other things someone can find on old studio tapes in a couple of years and I can build a one-time-only stadium show every second year that will last until I'm too old to move.

"I want to live in the place I bought on that Caribbean island and do my painting and sculpture. I've got a showing in that gallery in the states that Jorgensson says is mostly sold before it opens!

"I never liked performing in a routine situation. I don't need the money and have no life of my own anymore.

"We're booked for six more shows and go on hiatus. I'll stay out except for special deals. I'm burning out and know it. I won't be one of those pathetic used-to-be types who tour until they're eighty on the strength of one old hit."

"Oh, come *on!*" Frank Lorner, her agent, cried. "You'll get three or four hits from this album and the crap you'll leave laying around will produce hits for the next ten years!"

"Exactly!" she retorted. "Why do the touring bit? Why drive myself to exhaustion when I'll probably do better if I handle it this way?

"My mind's made up. I've got fifty seven songs here. Let's pick a few and do the studio tape runthroughs with whatever will hold up." She dropped the sheaf of songs she'd written on the table.

"... you left me, Baby. I just wanted to say 'thanks!'" Mar finished. The crowd, those who weren't standing already,

## *Final Tour*

stood to wildly cheer the latest platinum hit from her "Final Tour" album. She waved tiredly, said, "Goodbye all! It's been quite a decade, hasn't it?" and exited the stage. The band tried to play over the noise, but it wasn't working so she went back to the mike to pick up her acoustic guitar and held her hand up for silence – which she got.

"I didn't plan to come back, but I thought of a song on my way off the stage and want to try it out here," she announced. "If you promise to bear with me through the mistakes I'll sit here – if Arch will get me a stool? – and try to write it.

"You have to promise to not do this to me anymore if I do."

The crowd roared in agreement.

She sat on the stool, tuned the guitar and said, "I said, 'It's been quite a decade' when I left before and that made me think of this." She tried a few chords and settled on "C" for the ease of playing a high counterpoint melody on a "G" matrix overlay.

"I came onto the scene, scared, young and green and hoped my voice would hold out for the show.

"That was a full decade ago.

"Forward two years, during which I faced my fears and learned that I had something more to say.

"White Witch Woman, Devil of A Man" gave me a name. The tours began and I've never had a time to rest. I always believed that a singer must only give her best.

"Yes, it's been quite a decade.

"Ten years ago today.

"People say I've had it made and I guess that's true.

"Well, time runs out for all of us, our seasons in the sun and rain, glitter and pain, in one short moment become part of the past.

"But it really was quite a decade.

"Ten years ago today."

She made up the words as she sang, which was her talent, and told the entire story in a bit more than six minutes, then waved to the audience and exited the stage. This time they knew absolutely she wouldn't return.

There was a man standing outside the bus door in the rain. A man in a silver/tan trench coat and Homburg hat, of all things. She didn't need anymore problems and had a lot of experience with overly persistent fans – but there was no way any fan could get out there. Security was tight.

She wished she had let Arnie, the door guard, walk her out, but didn't expect to find anyone there.

She couldn't stand in the rain to consider so ran on.

The man was certainly handsome! He had the strangest eyes! They seemed to glow.

He opened the door to the bus as she got there and stood back for her to enter. She stopped just inside and asked who he was and what he wanted from her.

"Merlin Tyana. I'm a crime analyst," the stranger replied. "May I speak with you?"

"Crime analyst? What does ... I mean, come on in," she answered. "I don't...?"

He removed the Homburg and she felt a bit dizzy, again noting she had never seen a man quite so handsome and his thick, wavy mahogany hair somehow fit him, as did the trench coat – and even the Homburg.

"Oh, it's not so much to do with you," Merlin said, smiling with perfect teeth. "It has more to do with the business and with people you've met, some in other fields."

"I don't...?" she replied.

"A Mister Lars Jorgensson, in Los Angeles?" Merlin said.

"Oh. Him. The art?" she replied. "He has an art gallery

*Final Tour*

there that sold some of my things. They brought ten times what I thought they would and he kept very careful records, so there was no theft or anything."

"Have you sent more since?" Merlin asked.

"Well, no. Not yet. I have twenty four paintings and six sculptures packaged. They'll go out on Monday a week," she answered.

"I'm amazed you have the time to do that work with your full touring schedule," Merlin said. "You're retiring as of tonight?"

"Well, there are things we've recorded that were never released so I'll probably be forced to do a show or two a year, which is part ... I'll be honest. We have all that planned. The stuff'll be 'found' by accident every couple of years.

"I only sleep for three or four hours a night except after a show, so do the art bit then."

"How did you ever manage to find an art agent in the states and not here?" he asked.

"Oh, Frank – Frank Lorner, my agent – found him and made the deals. He said the price there would be a lot more than here – and that's certainly been true!"

"I suppose you can devote a lot of time to art now," Merlin suggested. "You seem to be prolific in everything you do. You've written more than two hundred songs in ten years and did all the art things at the same time."

"I have a hideaway on a small island in the Caribbean," she said. "I can now devote all my time to whatever I want to do, so there will be a lot more paintings. I already have plans on a series and the same with the sculptures."

"The band will hate to see you go, I imagine," he said. "Frank will be able to book them. He'll have connections with a number of other people, no doubt, being a popular enough agent to have managed you.

"I guess what comes in in royalties will be a good living for all of you for years. He'll get his cut of what you've done and the band will get theirs.

"Since you've retired the music will bring in big money, but the art will suffer if you do much of it."

"I never thought of that and don't really care," she replied. "I have more than I'll ever need.

"Frank did seem very upset about the art and has tried to get me to go slow, but that's not my nature. I'm his only talent, but that's because I'm a fulltime project until now and the art will keep him going for years. He's already made a lot more than most agents will ever hope to see. Kyle wants to keep the band going and we'll get married because we both want a family, but we're both music freaks so know we'll spend a lot of time apart. We're used to it.

"The stories about musicians and wild sex parties are vastly exaggerated. A front, like me, would have the time and energy, but a touring band spends all its time moving.

"I have the art to fill my time and never was one to look for relationships. I've always had one lover for a long period and Kyle's the same. We're neither one angels, but we're not nearly as bad as the publicity.

"Lord! I never discuss personal matters and can't understand why I am with you!

"Why are you here, Mr. Tyana?

"Merlin," he answered. "Because of some strange hints I've received and the fact that the music and art will be worth a much larger fortune if you're ... not around, and because I've heard you've had a few close calls lately. Accidents that almost happened except for your quickness and good luck.

"There have been some rather strange accidents among

clients of ... certain people ... whenever it appears the ... well, I mostly want to make it absolutely certain you've taken proper ... precautions."

"Precautions? I ... Whatever do you mean?" she asked, becoming a bit alarmed at the danger suggestion and the mysterious manner in which Merlin was trying to say something without saying it.

"Well, if I might be so bold as to suggest you arrange that if anything happens to you all art unsold at the time will be returned and donated to a charity of your choice and the same should be true of any songs or material not released at the time of your ... unavailability.

"I'm sure you'll want to protect the band, somehow. Perhaps stating they are to receive normal royalties from the music and can renew the copyrights in the name of the band."

"Well ... Merlin, you're scaring me!" she cried. "Should I include Frank?"

"Very definitely *not*!" Merlin retorted sharply. "Be sure he and that Jorgensson character are cut off completely and be sure they both know it.

"I very seldom am this blunt with people, but you seem a very strong person and I doubt there is much time. You have to be very careful and you have to watch your back, so to speak."

"I was a bit worried about that set that fell," she agreed, thinking. "The car that almost hit me in Paris seemed a bit odd, seeing it went so far out of the lane and it didn't stop. That PA amplifier shorting out while we were rehearsing ... it's a good thing we were experimenting with a broadcast mike. If it had been a cord.... It IS a little too much, isn't it? Frank's the one who said we shouldn't report it because we didn't need the negative publicity.

## *Final Tour*

"You see, I *do* have a few suspicions of my own, but I thought maybe it was another ... someone else. Someone who didn't want anyone actually hurt, but who wanted publicity that would hold the band together. That's why June Lake was let go, frankly. She was my publicist and she has no ... sense of proportion."

"Well, I've warned you and I have to go," Merlin said. "Be careful. Get things set to where it won't do them any good to do you real harm."

She nodded and watched as he replaced the hat, smiled at her and stepped out. She thought a few seconds, then went to the door to call a question to him, but he wasn't anywhere in sight on the large, empty lot.

She shrugged to herself and went back inside to the kitchenette to heat the coffee. She smelled gas, so didn't light the burner. She looked at the propane tank and saw the fitting wasn't tight and was leaking. If she'd lit that burner the whole place might have exploded!

She'd made coffee before the show so that coupling had to have been loosened during the time she was appearing onstage. Deliberately.

Most people would have been frightened by it. It merely angered her.

"OK. Here's the way it goes," Marlene told the assembled group. "I've spent the morning with a pack of lawyers and this is set in stone so don't bother to argue.

"I'm not stupid and I resent being treated as if I were. I had to know about all the little almost-accidents that have been happening the past two months weren't accidents, so let's not pretend.

"Guys, I know my band had nothing to do with it. I've

arranged for you to get full royalties on anything we did together the rest of your lives.

"If anything happens to me, any accident that causes me to be unable to continue with *any* of my projects, either because of a disability or death, all royalties from sales and use are to go to the band.

"All art not sold is to be given immediately to the UN AIDS Task Force to be used as they see fit. All properties and monies, stocks and anything else is to go to my sisters and brother, split equally, unless I'm married or have children at the time.

"These stipulations are to be part of any and all future contracts and agreements made by me or in my name.

"Any questions?"

"Perhaps you should not act too hastily," Frank said. "The way that was stated I get nothing! I'm sure that was an oversight?"

"No. I have no need of an agent anymore," Mar answered. "You already have a couple million dollars from managing the business and I'm now retired from the business. Lawyers will handle the details now."

"But what about all the leftover studio tapes and tours?" he demanded.

"I'll book the tours myself and the band can handle their own business," she pointed out. "Kyle does half the booking already, so why pay you to hang on?

"You didn't think I knew that, did you? You didn't know I kept an eye on things while you were spending so much of your time in the states the past two years.

"I should have given you the boot back when that started, but the decision to retire was already made so I let you stay.

"No. If anything happens to me you and your friends are

*Final Tour*

out of it. Period."

He wanted to say something more, but didn't dare. He suddenly looked very scared and ran out into the drizzle, almost knocking Merlin Tyana, who was just coming to the door, down. Merlin asked what spooked that strange man. He looked like he'd seen a ghost.

Marlene told him she'd told Frank he was out and introduced the band.

"You told him and he suddenly raced out like that?" Merlin asked. "Maybe someone should see where he goes?"

Kyle looked grim, nodded and dodged out the door to see Frank just entering the arena building. He raced after him, then Dan Johns went to back up Kyle. Marlene picked up the phone to call security.

"I saw him go into the business offices, but there were a lot of people wandering around there so he went up to the dressing room," Kyle explained. "I saw him coming out so was able to hide in the storage closet. Dan was behind me and stayed to follow him in case he didn't go to the dressing rooms.

"He came in and looked around, then went to the telephone and opened an outside line. I had a shelf full of recorders in there so turned one on and got this."

He switched on a portable tape recorder and ran it back, then switched "Play" on.

Frank: "Come on! Come on! Answer, damn it! Pick up the damned ... Mr. Smith? Frank Jones.

"The deal is off! Do *not* make the hit! Something has come up and we're all dead meat if it comes off!"

Pause.

Frank: "Oh, Dear God! You have to stop it!"

Pause.

Frank: "Tonight? This morning later or ... NO! NOT NOW! Oh, dear God! I have to get out of here! If he kills her now we're all going to spend the rest of our lives locked ... I have to get ... What are *you* doing here?"

Kyle: "Busting your miserable stinking damned ass!" There was a crash, then silence.

"I knocked the slimy bastard across the desk and Dan came in and pulled me off of him," Kyle said. "Arnie came running in and held him for the police. The number he called was right there so his 'Mr. Smith' will be picked up.

"Something is planned for right away. Mar is coming with me and the rest of you watch your asses. I have a car right outside the door so we can stick together if you like."

They agreed and quickly got into the SUV Kyle borrowed from Arnie and headed for a hotel downtown.

"Wait!" Mar cried as they got in the SUV. "Merlin can ride with us ... where is he?"

He was nowhere to be seen in the large empty lot.

"Harold Simmons was arrested with a propane tank bomb as he was placing it under the bus used by the band, *Able Bodies*, this morning before daylight," the news commentator on the Morning TV News said. "Police had staked out the tour bus on a tip that a security guard, Arnold Baskins, gave them when he detained the agent for the band, Franklin Lorner, explaining that Lorner had made a telephone call to a known criminal to set up the crime.

"Marlene Able, the lead singer and songwriter for the band, retired last evening from touring to promote her music, saying she wished to concentrate on her painting and sculpture...."

"I really don't get *why*!" Dan said.

"Because a painting by a dead artist with huge talent is worth a thousand times what the same painting is worth if the artist is turning out a new one every week," Kyle replied. "What I'll never understand in this life is what happened to that Merlin character! There was no way he could have gotten out of sight in so little time! He simply disappeared into thin air!"

"Whatever, I'm damned glad he was there!" Mar declared.

"Amen," the others agreed.

## *Pictures*

Laura Thurston checked her purse again, then sighed.

Where did she leave her wallet? She hadn't taken it out of the purse at the party.

She didn't want to believe that Ann Mills or her friends would steal anything. There hadn't been any money in the wallet. Just business cards, her date list, a few pictures. A Visa card.

Her driver's license, but no one could use that. Her pictures, even the ones on the driver's license, looked like her and she was distinctive enough that no one could pass themselves off as her.

She was uncomfortable enough at that party, what with Allen Damson being there with Carole Francis and Gail Winton giving them all her hard look. She was totally out of place there and that made the rest of the guests very uncomfortable. Ann had apologized profusely to Laura and explained, in private, that she thought that Gail would be like everyone else and accept that Allen was Allen and always would be. Thanks for the yuks and see you around.

Gail and Allen had been an "item" only a few months ago and he had dropped her and dated Laura for awhile. She didn't know he had been anyone's "steady" at the time because he was dating anyone who would spare him the time, which she learned very quickly. She had cut that off as soon as she found out. Carole had stepped right in. Allen was a bit shocked that anyone would dump him because he had always been the dumper and never the dumpee. He was a bit miffed, but soon took it in stride.

Well, Allen had a certain charm and was quite goodlooking.

*Pictures*

Carole would learn soon enough that he wasn't going to be around long.

Ann had introduced her to Allen, but it was just one of those passing things. They had once dated in a semi-serious way and were good friends. They got together now and then for laughs and liked a lot of the same things. He had come into the restaurant where they were having lunch, she had introduced them and it had gone on from there. Ann had even warned her not to get serious because Allen was very definitely not the type who would.

Bill Goodwin had come with Gail so she should have had the decency not to act like that – but he was a last-minute date. Ann threw parties on impulse and it was pure chance she didn't have a date planned or Laura wouldn't have been there herself. She had mentioned to Ann that she and Donny Alred had planned to go to the opening at the new Parks Theater, but he had to cancel at the last minute because of an emergency operation.

Donny was a surgeon. A damned good one.

Ann said her own date had the flu so she would call a bunch of friends and they could have a Happy Nothing Day Party. She wasn't that involved with Aaron anyhow. He was too selfcentered for her tastes, far too possessive and she was planning to dump him soon. Maybe she would meet someone nice at the party. She'd tell everyone to bring whoever they liked, the more the merrier!

Well, every party had a pooper. Laura had taken Ann's advice and ignored Gail and it wasn't really that bad. She did have a little fun with most of the people there. Aaron Gladstone, Ann's soon-to-be-dumped boyfriend showed up late and was a little drunk. Laura saw what Ann meant about the possessive type. He seemed to think it was all right for

*Pictures*

him to "hit" on Laura, but was jealous if Ann talked to any man other than him. He flirted with Gail from the first second Ann introduced them and she seemed to go for it, probably only to try to make Allen jealous. He wouldn't care.

Gail left with Bill so he would take her home and leave her there, the way she had acted. She tried to make Allen jealous, insulted the one she came with and her flirtation got her less than nothing because Aaron was the type to see if he could do something. He wouldn't actually do it because that would give Ann a weapon to hold over him and he was the possessive one. The rest of the people there left just at midnight and she went out almost last, at the same time Allen and Carole left, chatting with them in the lift to the ground floor. Allen dropped her at her apartment, saving her cab fare, which was ridiculous for the three squares to her place. She didn't want to walk home alone after midnight and Carole saw she wasn't competition for Allen.

She sighed again. She'd mention the lost wallet to Ann tomorrow. Maybe it would turn up. Someone might have slipped it out of the purse and taken it somewhere else to open it and find there was no money in it.

She would call and cancel the Visa card as soon as she got inside. She could re-install it when she got it back.

"Miss Thurston?" the police officer asked when she opened the door at dawn the following day (She was stock manager at Flock's and had to be there at seven so there was nothing unusual about the early hour to her. She was always up well before six). "Miss Laura Thurston?"

"Yes?" she replied, and looked quizzically at him and the two other policemen there.

"I am Inspector Milkins, CID," he said. "Would you come

*Pictures*

with us, please? We have to ask you a few questions.

"You might wish to have an attorney present."

"What in the world?" Laura asked, confused.

"We'll explain everything when down at the yard," he answered. "Please cooperate. I wish to avoid having to arrest you here."

She said to come in. He would have to arrest her if he wasn't going to let her call the office and put on some clothes. He said that was fair enough and sat on her sofa while she changed and called her boss to say she would be late. She put the breakfast away and locked the place, then went with Milkins and the two silent officers to New Scotland Yard where they asked again if she wanted an attorney.

"How would I know?" she replied. "I don't know why we're here! I'd think you could at least tell me that!"

"Oh, yes, I see. We're investigating the Aaron Gladstone murder," Milkins explained sternly. "You have a lot of explaining to do!"

"Aaron Gladstone? You mean Ann Mills' latest flop?" Laura said with a grimace. "He was at the party last.... Excuse me? MURDER?"

"How did your wallet get inside his apartment, Miss Thurston?" Milkins demanded.

"My wallet? It was taken at the party," she answered. "If it was in his apartment he must have taken it."

"It was stolen at a party? You mentioned that to others at the time?" Milkins asked. "That will go far toward substantiating your story. It will make several others come under scrutiny."

"I didn't know it was missing until I got home and looked in the purse for my keys," Laura explained. "I was going to call Ann this morning and ask her about it."

"Very convenient," Milkins said dryly.

"Okay! That did it!" Laura snarled. "I've tried to cooperate with you and all it gets me is ... is.... I want the lawyer now.

"I did call Visa this morning to cancel the card and tell them it was missing if that means anything.

"The cooperation part is over. That remark was totally uncalled-for!"

"Miss Thurston, we have some very convincing evidence you were at his apartment and that you may have killed him. I must warn you that your actions will be most carefully considered," Milkins snapped back at her. "If you aren't guilty I suggest that you don't act as though you are!"

"Then arrest me," she replied. "I'll talk to you again only after my attorney advises me!"

"I won't arrest you quite yet," he replied. "You may go, but you will be watched. Carefully!"

"*You* will return me to my apartment!" she said. "You brought me here and you'll take me back home!"

"Oh? Do you own a handgun, Miss Thurston?" he asked.

She stared at him.

"We'll check the registry," he said pointedly.

"Do that!" she shot back. "It's what you're paid to do, isn't it?

"Are you going to take me home in the police car or are you paying for a cab?"

He grinned and shook his head, then yelled, "Albert!" and had the officer drive her home. Albert said Milkins wasn't half as bad as he seemed. He got a lot of criminals to make a slip that caught them with his act.

"Did he pull that, 'The knife seems to be very much like the one people saw you with,' line? Or the 'What were you doing

*Pictures*

on Hampton Lane last evening?' one?"

"No, but I wouldn't fall for it, anyhow," Laura said. "Is that where his apartment is? Hampton Lane? He was stabbed?"

"I don't know for sure which one he's handling," Albert admitted. "I just said Hampton Lane because it popped into mind."

"I don't even know where his apartment is and Inspector Milkins said something about me owning a handgun, which I don't," Laura said. "Maybe that was his trick?"

"No, that tells him something else," Albert answered. "I'd say he has something that ties you to it pretty tight, but he doesn't believe it for some reason. If he has something solid and you're not in a cell right now he doesn't believe you did it. He's pretty good with his hunches. Usually right on the money.

"Be careful. If somebody's trying to make you look guilty it could work. I've seen it."

"Thanks. I will," Laura promised and got out at her apartment stoop. She decided to go to the restaurant down the block for coffee and a snack. She hadn't eaten anything yet.

Damn! It was going to pour!

Well, she could claim she was trapped in the restaurant all morning by the rain and her boss would accept that. She didn't much feel like going to work today.

The rain came in buckets just as she reached the restaurant door. She dodged inside to find the place almost empty except for an older couple at one table and a man at a table to the side where she liked to sit.

She was going to another table when the man looked up and smiled at her. She couldn't help but notice he was extremely handsome in a movie idol kind of way. He even had a trench coat and Homburg hat on the rack next to the table!

*Pictures*

"Care for company?" he asked. "I'm not trying to pick you up, but there's no point in us taking up separate tables and neither having anyone to talk with.

"If I'm presumptuous don't be afraid to tell me so. I'm a gregarious sort by nature.

"Merlin Tyana. Just Merl."

A sudden bright flash of lightning made his eyes shine strangely in the deeper shadows of the Schefflera where he was sitting. He had the thickest dark mahogany hair and perfect teeth, but seemed a bit indistinct in the shadows where the lightning competed with the much softer fluorescent lights of the restaurant. If he was trying to pick her up it was definitely going to work. He was a very magnetic sort.

"Laura Thurston, latest suspected coldblooded murderer," she replied. "I could use someone to talk to. You may be taking your life in your own hands to invite me to your table! Be warned!"

"Oh? You killed someone?" Merl asked. "You seem a purposeful sort.

"Who did you kill and why?"

"According to Inspector Milkins, a man named Aaron Gladstone," she answered. "They haven't told me why."

"Ah! Gladstone!" Merl said. "I can't think of why anyone would want to kill him other than the old 'I could just KILL him!' thing.

"What does the sneaky Inspector Milkins have that makes him think you did it?"

"You know Milkins?" Laura asked. "Someone stole my wallet at a little party last night, then it turns up in his apartment with his body – or something."

"And you were at his apartment because?" Merl asked. "I'm a bit of an analyst with murder cases. Don't answer anything

*Pictures*

you don't think is any of my business."

"I don't even know where his apartment is," Laura protested. "I only met him last night and only saw him from a distance a time or two before that. He was dating a friend.

"You're an analyst? What does that mean?"

"I stand back from a crime and see what I can see," Merl answered. "People who are directly involved are usually too close to see the whole picture and I can sometimes spot something.

"Tell me about it. Maybe I'll spot something."

"It would appear your Mr. Gladstone was killed entirely to serve as a method to get you convicted of murder," Merl concluded. "Who has a motive to want you out of the way?"

"No one who I can think of," Laura answered. "There just doesn't seem to be any point to it!"

"There's always a point," Merl said. "Knowing the sneaky way Milkin does things you can be quite sure Gladstone wasn't killed with a gun or knife. Your being here means he's quite sure you didn't do it. He's actually a very effective investigator."

"What do you mean?" Laura asked. "He asked about a handgun, but it was Albert who said something about a knife."

"Good cop, bad cop," Merl replied. "It's their routine.

"We can't come up with a motive very well. At least, not against you."

"Well, talking with you has got me thinking," Laura said. "See what you think of this.

"Gail was going with Allen and I came along. She could think I took him away from her.

"She flirted with Gladstone last night, then went home with

*Pictures*

Bill, who was insulted with the way she was acting so probably dropped her off and told her to ... you know.

"She had a few drinks. I took her boyfriend. Aaron played her for a fool. She went to get her things and my purse was right there. She took the wallet, went home, then went to Aaron's place and killed him, planted my wallet and went back home.

"She would get even with both of us that way!"

"Didn't you say she was introduced to him at the party and that she left before you and he was still there when you left?" Merl asked. "I suppose he might have told her where he lived.

"I can see a woman wanting to set another woman up who had taken a lover away from her, but killing some jerk she met at a party and flirted with a few minutes, as you said, to make the former boyfriend jealous, doesn't fit unless she's a psycho.

"This seems to have been set up carefully and that doesn't fit her killing someone she met at a party earlier that night. She couldn't have even known he would be there.

"Who else had a strong enough motive, even if from a warped perspective? Who else had lost a boyfriend or girlfriend or money or something? Who was in position to set it up? Who was there every step of the way?

"I'm sure Milkins will be able to figure it. He's sneaky, but he's also very good at his job. He gets you so angered at his put-on arrogant attitude that you slip up.

"Well, the rain's letting up and I'm supposed to be working so I'm afraid I have to leave your very pleasant company.

"Take care – and don't be bluffed by Milkins."

He stood, took his hat and trench coat from the rack, smiled a dazzling smile at her and left. She stared hard at the table

*Pictures*

for a few seconds, then a little gasp/snarl escaped her. She looked up to call to Merl that she had it figured, but he seemed to be gone already.

She was surprised to see it was hardly past seven thirty! It seemed she'd been up for hours!

"Milkins, I have this one figured out," Laura announced. "No games. You and Albert play that one on someone else.

"How was he killed?"

"With the good old-fashioned fireplace poker," Milkins answered. "He was in bed and someone smacked him a total of seven times across the head. Viciously. Who did it?"

"It was planned over a period of time, wouldn't you agree?" she asked.

"Not necessarily," he argued. "If you got PO'ed at him you could have picked up the poker and did him in. Spur of the moment kind of thing." He grinned.

"I'm not the type," she countered. "Let's not play games. You know very well there's only one person in this world who could have set this up."

"Miss Thurston, you have a lot of information about the people there last night that I don't have, so enlighten me," Milkins suggested.

She explained the same way she'd explained to Merl. Milkins thought for a minute, then nodded with a grim look on his face.

"One problem, how do we prove it?" he asked. "He was there when everyone else was gone and he was found this morning in bed in his apartment. He was drunk at her party so she took him home. Only she would be there after he went to bed. She set it up when you said you didn't have a date all of a sudden.

*Pictures*

"As you said, planned. The Gail woman wasn't the only one who felt you took away a boyfriend and her present one was awfully possessive and wasn't going to be easy to dump, so he ends up dead, you're accused and her old boyfriend and now good platonic friend comforts her at the loss of her lover. I disagree with that. She's not a psycho. She's cold and calculating. How do we prove it?"

"Why, the same way you two generally do it," Laura replied. "Get her mad and make her slip up.

"I can make a plan, too!"

"Well, dear! I'm glad they've let you go, but how could they think you didn't ... I mean, what changed their mind about you?" Ann asked, adjusting the towel around her wet hair.

"Oh, they don't have anything but a wallet that I'd reported missing to the Visa company," Laura said offhandedly. "It might also be helpful if I'd spent the time after I left the party with someone who could say I wasn't wherever Aaron lived.

"You shouldn't wash your hair at night. It won't dry and will smell. I'd lend you my drier, but it's back at my place.

"Good lord! It's only eight ten?! It seems like *hours!*

"I'm sorry. I know you don't usually get up before nine or so, but I'm run a little ragged this morning."

"Oh? Was your hunk back from his doctoring?" Ann asked, not paying attention to the rest of it.

"No. It was another old friend. It seems they can't honestly suspect anyone who was with someone else and they were together for hours," Laura said flippantly, with a bit of a sneer. "They also have to consider if Aaron's neighbor said there was someone else at his place he saw come in and can remember the car and the person. Someone who's been there before so it would be easy to find them – and I don't even have a car."

"Neighbor? There's no one up in that place at that time ... I mean, that could be a real break!" Ann cried, suddenly nervous. "The car? He saw them in a car?"

"Yeah. Some neighbor had a fight with his wife and was sleeping in his car or something," Laura replied. "I'd better get to work! I'll be late enough today and Gordy's not going to let that go on forever!

"Let's plan another party soon! You're free to find someone worth the bother!" She waved airily and went out to sit across the street with Milkins. Ann came out in less than five minutes and went into the apartment parking garage. After another three minutes Albert called them over the walky-talky. Ann had gone to a Taurus parked in the visitors' spaces and opened the boot to take out a plastic rain poncho and some wet clothes.

"It was a car that belonged to a friend who is in France for a few days. She had use of it," Milkins explained. "Seems Gladstone was killed in a very bloody way, which is why I knew you didn't have anything to do with it from the start. There wouldn't be any way you would invite me into your apartment to nose around while you changed if you'd been there in that bloody a scene that recently.

"As you said, it was planned. She had the poncho and a sort of laboratory smock thing and a pair of old boots in the boot to get rid of after we'd searched everything around here. It had blood on it. Lots of blood. Gladstone's blood. You noted that she'd had a shower in the early morning hours to wash off the spatters.

"Now. Tell me how you figured it so fast."

"Let's say I had someone who very cleverly steered me into stepping back and looking at the whole picture," Laura said.

*Pictures*

"He said when one's too close all she sees is bits and pieces.

"There really was no one else it could have been."

"But you came up with the plan to catch her," Milkins pointed out.

"Sneaky. I had a good teacher," Laura replied.

"Oh? Who would that be?" Milkins wondered.

"You," Laura said.

"Could be!" he agreed.

## *Well, Well*

"Oh, John! It's just *perfect*!" Lana Klington cried as her fiancee, John Wright, showed her the pictures of the picturesque cabin by the lake. "We can dream about it, but we could never afford it.

"How did you ever find it?"

"It was one of the places listed in a flyer my Uncle Fred had dropped on his stoop in Kennerly and it's right in our price range," John replied happily. "It's one of those places with no facilities in place, but Uncle Fred will help us with running in the electric and there's a well already there with a pitcher pump on it. We can attach an electric and I can run the plumbing in myself. I worked with Rogers' Plumbing for more than two years and even have a journeyman certificate!

"All else will be a septic tank and it's approved out there because it's more than six meters above the lake level and has good percolation in that sand."

"Percolation? I don't know what that is, but I'll take your word for it," she said. "It's just so *perfect*! And we both can handle our jobs from anywhere with the comps! The phone line will come in with the electric, I suppose. We'll need two. Maybe three for the business and a personal line.

"Please don't ever mention Rogers again. I don't care if I never hear the name the rest of my life!" She had been engaged to Rodney Rogers before she met John and he had been a monster who wanted to own her and control her every move. She had to keep a permanent restraining order against him when he stalked her after she escaped his abuse.

"Percolation. Drainage," John said. "I can get everything done in my spare time and we can move in the tenth of next month. It'll be our permanent honeymoon house!"

"Oh, John! I truly love it – and I love you so!" she cried.

"Well, it's done!" John announced on the eighth as he sat at a back table in The Minstrel's Retreat to wait out the thunderstorm outside. "I hooked up the well pump and pressure tank today, the septic's in and approved, the electric and phone are on – and there was already a bottled gas furnace so I put in a gas stove. If the electric goes out in a storm we can still cook.

"Two days from this moment I'll be carrying you across the threshold into our dream house!

"You're going to totally love that place. I already do. I've deliberately kept you away so it can be a new place for us to start a new life together.

"I got the Denniston account solid and it starts on the fifteenth so we'll be pretty well set. It's a very good income in itself and it won't take but a third of my time. I can keep most of my other accounts."

"Oh, John! It's so *perfect*!" Lana cried.

"Excuse me?" a tall man in a trench coat and (of all things!) a Homburg hat said. "I hate to intrude, but this place is so crowded and your third seat is the only one left?"

"Oh, join us! Do!" Lana replied. "We've just arranged for a perfect life together and I so want to tell someone about it! Be warned! I'll happy-talk you to death!"

He smiled broadly with perfect teeth as he removed the Homburg, exposing thick, rich, wavy mahogany hair. Lana was almost shocked at how handsome he was.

"That sounds a pleasant way to go!" he replied, taking the seat. "I get very little happy-talk in my profession.

"What makes your life so perfect?"

## Well, Well

Lana tried to look into the strange glowing dark eyes, but the lightning reflections made it hard to focus. There was something indistinct about the man. "We're getting married tomorrow. We have the perfect place to live. Our financial future is solid.

"I'm Lana and he's John. Soon to be Mr. and Mrs. John Wright.

"What's wrong with your profession?"

"Merlin Tyana. Just Merl," the man answered. "There's nothing wrong with the profession, it's just not a very happy one. I'm a criminal analyst. Murder."

John laughed. "Oh, really? Do you mean criminal analyst or criminal analyst?" he asked. Lana slapped him playfully on the shoulder and said, "You're *awful*!"

Merl joined the laughter and replied that he didn't have the bent to be a criminal, but enjoyed puzzles. He was often amazed at how people involved in a situation could only see little bits and pieces while he could step back and view the whole picture.

"There are too many times when people overlook a coincidence that isn't a coincidence," he explained. "They fail to believe that something that is too good to be true is usually too good to be true. There is a lot of truth in the old adage that one must always remember that a bed of roses has thorns.

"So many times there is a clue when something is not as it should be and spotting that clue can make the dream a reality."

John was suddenly nervous. "Are you saying we'd better step back and look our gift horse in the mouth?" he asked.

"Oh! I didn't ... I wasn't speaking of your... it was a general comment," Merl protested. "If any such coincidences appeared in your great good fortune I'm sure you've investigated them."

"No, quite frankly, we haven't," John said. "I do tend to a bit of cynicism about life and have had the feeling that all this is too good to be true."

"Oh, John! Don't ruin it!" Lana pleaded.

"Perhaps a little analysis can make the dream a reality," Merl suggested. "As I stated, if the coincidences can be explained the reality can be the dream.

"So! What coincidences have you encountered? Let's dispose of them here and now, then you can get on with the dream."

"Well, that flyer where Uncle Fred told me about the place when nobody else seemed to have gotten one," John replied. "It struck me as odd that I'm the only one who answered it when the place was such an obvious bargain.

"Of course, it may be Uncle Fred helping us. He'd be the type to do that, I think. Set it up to give us a good start. That's really the only thing that seems ... contrived, if you know what I mean."

"Well, it's most probably exactly that," Merlin replied. "A wealthy uncle might very well, as you say, contrive to arrange that you receive an expensive helping hand from somewhere unbeknownst to you.

"If that's the only coincidence, greet your good fortune and the love of your uncle gladly."

"Oh!" Lana cried. "Uncle Fred isn't wealthy. He's a pensioner – an adequate pension, but he's not wealthy by any standard."

"Then he may have arranged the gift through someone else," Merlin suggested. "If that's all I wouldn't worry.

"Tell me about the place."

## *Well, Well*

John explained about the place, its isolation and how he had to arrange for all facilities, the septic system and the well pump and tank, plus making the old wood stove into a gas stove.

"It's very well-built and solid," he finished. "Even in its isolation its location above the lake and the amount of land and considering it had no facilities it would be worth more than a hundred thousand pounds, yet we got it for fifty six thousand and Uncle Fred helped to his limits with running in the electric and that sort of thing."

"It's a bit unusual, but not unheard of, for such a place to go for a pittance," Merlin agreed. "Perhaps a divorce settlement where the husband sold it at minimum to keep the scheming ex-wife from getting a lot of money he worked for. Perhaps an inheritance by someone who doesn't look forward to isolation. A city person. There are a lot of explanations. Such things do happen.

"The thing I find strange is that you say no one else made a competing bid. It would seem a real estate holding company would be anxious to obtain such a place as investment. They would work on a margin of perhaps fifteen percent and you got it at little more than half.

"It's strange, but I can see no sinister reason anyone would arrange such a thing. It would have to be directed at you and only you. Unless there is someone who wants to do either or both of you harm for any reason it seems more a stroke of exceptional good fortune than anything else."

"Oh, dear God!" Lana wailed. "Rodney! He could do something like that. He has an awful lot of money.

"Why? To get me into an isolated place?"

She explained about Rodney Rogers and the abuse and stalking.

## Well, Well

"Perhaps you could trace the former ownership of the place to find if he was directly involved in it," Merlin suggested, thinking. "If he was your great good fortune holds because you have the place and can thwart his using its isolation to his advantage. It would seem a fitting irony that his scheme to bring harm to you would result in your achieving of one of your dreams."

"I have the papers on the place in my briefcase," John suggested, taking the leather case from beneath the table. "I didn't look at anything except the agents title guarantees, insurance, tax base – incidentally, taxes are very low because of the selling price – and the legal description of the land.

"Hmm. It seems Warfield Gerstein left it to his sister, Tanika Gerstein. There doesn't seem to be anything else – uh-oh!"

"Uh-oh?" Merl asked.

"Tanika. It's a very unusual name," John said.

"John! Rodney's *mother* was Tanika and she died less than two months ago!" Lana cried. "Oh, Merl, I'm getting very frightened!"

"There's no way that crud could come around that place where we wouldn't know it," John said. "The house has trees close, but it's in a meadow on a knoll, otherwise. We can put in a few of those motion detectors and nothing bigger than a hare could get anywhere near the house without an alarm.

"It doesn't make any sense!"

"He would know about that stuff. You can buy motion detectors at a home supply house," Merlin agreed. "It would have to be something in the house. A secret passage, a tunnel, and that would be worse than obsessively strange."

"There's no tunnel. I was all around under the house," John insisted. "I put in the plumbing and electric. Rodney's in the

## Well, Well

plumbing and well business. It would have to be something there, but I don't see how it could be that. I did have the well tested and it's exceptionally good water. I put in all the piping and it's very good, clean, approved material. I put on the pump, which I bought from Lancer's which Rogers' supplies on the wholesale end, but that's as close as they got to anything used on the place."

"Well, if the well was tested and new materials were used from that point he didn't put anything in it and couldn't get anything introduced into the well after the pump was attached to the pipe," Merlin said. "It probably *is* merely a coincidence that his mother once owned the place. If anything were now to be found that was deliberately placed to harm you there he would be caught in a way no barrister alive could refute.

"I see the rain is letting up so I must be along. I've very greatly enjoyed your good company and wish you true contentment and peace. Vaya con dios, as the saying goes."

They soon said their goodbyes, John looking thoughtful. He looked up to call to Merlin that he just had an idea, but Tyana was nowhere to be seem. It didn't seem possible he had left the place already.

John told his idea to Lana, who agreed.

Either way, they would have their dream.

"Inspector, I told Tyana I had tested the well and that all materials were new and approved," John explained. "There was no way anything could be introduced to the well after the pump was attached, as he pointed out.

"The well and the piping was definitely safe – but there was one section that hadn't been tested. The pump and tank.

"The pump, itself, didn't have anyplace where anything

## Well, Well

could be placed to contaminate the water so there was only the tank itself if the water, indeed, was contaminated and that would be easy as it has a removable plate to allow for replacement and servicing of the air reservoir pressure bag, though that was also attached by the piping.

"If that tank was found contaminated it was because something was introduced before it was delivered to me. It was in the sealed crate when the truck dropped it off, ordered from Lancer's, who ordered it from Rogers', who shipped it directly.

"I noticed that Merl had covered everything except that tank and pump in his consideration and feel it was deliberate so I would test the water.

"That lump of arsenic was put into that tank at Rogers'. It couldn't have been done anywhere else. It was to be delivered directly to me at that address.

"I've explained about how we got the place and how Rodney was the only person in this world who would do anything deliberately to harm either my wife or myself. The jury saw that very clearly and that's why he's going to spend the next thirty years locked up. I could see they would certainly convict in their eyes as they filed out. His arrogance certainly didn't do him any good and that attitude of him getting away with anything because he has money doesn't, as they say stateside, play in Peoria.

"I had to replace all the piping I'd installed because I don't trust anything that ever was contaminated with arsenic, but that was a few hundred-odd pounds – very cheap, all things considered.

"As Tyana said, sometimes a wonderful irony results in the very person who would destroy the lives of others accomplishing their dreams for them!"

*Well, Well*

"Hmfpth!" Inspector Carlin replied. "This is three times I've come across this Merlin Tyana character and every time it's a case of a killer being thwarted.

"I've got to meet this one! Somehow, I doubt I ever will!"

John nodded wisely.

## Rest Stop

The rain was intense. Joanna Franklin decided to look for the next rest stop and pull over until it let up some. She was far too nervous already to be driving in this kind of weather. There were signs that the road ahead was steep and dangerous when wet and there was almost no traffic on it, mostly heading back toward London. She'd seen exactly one lorry the past eight or ten kilometers.

What could Arlene Baily have found about Justin Gothard that would make her call the woman who she'd declared she hated and be so secretive about it? Jo knew Justin was raised in that area, but he'd never mentioned anything out of the ordinary and most certainly hadn't seemed to be hiding anything.

Arlene was a little scary and Jo wouldn't consider going to such a place to meet her except she had said to go directly to the police station, so that part would be safe enough.

One thing was certain! Arlene had better not be making up some wild story – which she was prone to do – just to send her on a chase and aggravate her. Not in this kind of weather!

She couldn't picture her soon-to-be husband having ever been involved in some kind of crazy criminal scheme the way Arlene hinted she'd found in some little burg like Finley Under Lyle. She'd never heard of the place and had a hard time finding it on the map even with Arlene's directions. She liked to have never found Lyle on the map, much less Finley Under Lyle!

Well, another ten or so kilometers.

This was a hell of a way to spend her day off!

Ah! There was a rest stop ahead with facilities! She could

## Rest Stop

wait out the storm there.

Wasn't that Arlene's car 'way over to the side? It was the only one there and it looked like hers.

This was some kind of trick. Jo was suddenly very suspicious of what Arlene was up to. She wasn't about to go inside there if there was no one else around. That woman was capable of anything.

Maybe it wasn't Arlene's car. There was a man in a trench coat and Homburg hat standing in the doorway.

That may be just as bad. No one wore Homburg hats anymore.

A sudden bolt of blinding lightning very close made her decide she would chance his being alright. She couldn't drive in these conditions, that was sure! The weatherman had finally gotten it right when he said there were going to be severe storms in the mountains!

Jo parked, got her old brollie from between the seats and ran into the building, the man holding the door open for her.

Lord have mercy! He was handsome! Like those older movies where the hero was all man, clean and responsible, not like today when the hero was some unshaven bum with no morals.

The man swept off the Homburg, exposing rich, thick, wavy, dark mahogany hair and smiled with perfect teeth. Jo actually felt weak in the knees. She hadn't felt like that since she was introduced to that rock star, Rod Stewart, when she was just a silly teenager (Well, that was only four years ago).

"Rather unpleasant weather to have to drive," the man said. "I'm afraid the electric's off out here and it's a bit dark inside. I have a battery lantern so it won't be too bad.

"There's some girl inside, I believe. I saw her go in when I came from the facilities in back."

*Rest Stop*

His voice was a pleasant modulated baritone and his eyes almost glowed. Jo could just manage to speak. "I'm Joanna Franklin," she introduced. "If that's not your car sitting over there I think I'll know the woman inside. I'm supposed to meet her in Finley Under Lyle. At the police station."

"Police station? At Finley Under Lyle?" he replied. "There is no police station at Finley. There's not even one at Lyle. The closest one is at Makebridge. I'm from Watersham Under Makebridge, which is hardly more than Finley. Makebridge is about the size of Lyle, but is more central to a number of small villages – you can't call them towns – in the area.

"I'm Merlin Tyana. Merl."

Jo stared at Merlin a long moment and he looked at her quizzically in return.

"There isn't a police station?" she asked in a hiss. "What is she up to?

"Mr. Tyana, I'm scared!"

"Merl," he replied. "Let's step outside and around to the dry side. There's a table under a covering and we can discuss your situation there. Perhaps something is not right here."

"Hah! There's no 'perhaps' about it!" she said. "Maybe I'd better get in my car and go!"

"If someone in there wishes to do you harm she will simply find another way," Merlin replied. "Perhaps we can find a way to put a permanent end to her schemes. Expose her for what she is?

"I am forced to assume there's a family problem – or perhaps a man?"

"I didn't think so, but it could well be," Jo agreed. They sat at the table and Merlin asked her to explain what was happening. "I'm a criminal analyst and this has the earmarks

**Page 52**

of a tragedy in the making," he explained. "We may avert it.

"Tell me from the start. Why would another woman go to such measures to harm you and why would you come out here on the word of any such person?

"Begin with purely background information. How long you've known her, the history between you, any factors that may figure into it.

"You are an attractive woman. I may assume she isn't? That there is a longterm jealousy?"

"Arlene's rather goodlooking in a studied sort of way," Jo answered. "She has a problem in that she wants to control people. She wants to own people if what her ex-boyfriends say is true.

"She has a lot of *ex* boyfriends. They last about two weeks with her and she can't see that no one wants to be owned and ordered around.

"I would say that Arlene's physically attractive, but has an attitude that is very offputting.

"We met, oh, about three years ago. She was attending a computer course I'd enrolled in for the company where I work. You can't advance far anymore in business if you don't use comps.

"She was flirting with several of the men in the class and I liked one of them, an Andy O'Rourke. She seemed to be a fun type of person at the time and suggested we have a friendly contest to see who could get him.

"She already had made a date with him, which I didn't know then. He went with her exactly twice, then we dated a few times. He wasn't about to get into a relationship with only one woman and I'm not getting into a sexual relationship on a casual basis with anyone (with one possible exception, she added in her mind and blushed. Merlin seemed to read her mind and laughed).

"Anyhow, he told me she was a total controlling bitch and he hoped he never got tied up with anything like her again.

"We dated a few more of the same men and I always ended up with them telling me the same thing about her. She's oblivious to her personality and seemed to think I was deliberately trying to humiliate her, which is parsecs from the truth.

"We had a couple of nasty confrontations and she would always apologize and try to act like a friend, then would deliberately try to get some man to reject me for her.

"I think she obsessed about it. My present fiancee has put an end to the competition because he told me several of his best friends told him she was bad news walking and he wouldn't give her the time of day.

"I think the problem is that she's unstable and I'm going to marry Justin, which leaves her the loser all the way. She never had a man who would stay with her for long and I do. She seems to think I'm marrying Justin solely to humiliate her. She's been trying to find something to use as a wedge between Justin and me.

"She called me to meet her at the Finley Under Lyle police station because she'd found records there that Justin has a very serious criminal history.

"Justin was raised in this area."

"When did she call you?" Merlin asked.

"This morning," she replied.

"After she saw the road was as much as impassable and that this is the only rest stop on it," Merlin said. "There is very little traffic at the best of times so she could depend on not having anyone around when you came in to wait out the storm.

*Rest Stop*

"I was wondering why her car was parked so far to the side. It would seem a normal person would park as near the entrance as possible.

"Hmm. Let me call an old friend in the police department at Makebridge. Perhaps your Arlene will discover you're still one step ahead of her schemes!"

He took a cell phone from his coat pocket, dialed and handed it to her. She raised an eyebrow and he told her to tell the officer how she seemed to be set up for some kind of attack and that she wanted an officer here to go inside with her.

The officer said there was a cruiser only a kilometer away and that it would be there in five minutes or less. She handed Merlin the phone and told him the officer was on the way.

They went around front to wait and Jo was struck with an odd feeling that no time had passed since she got out of her car and came to the door. The sameness of the storm and the deserted road seemed to have suspended time somehow.

Jo suggested they wait in her car because Arlene might come to look out the door to see if she was there and it would ruin everything if they were standing there. Merlin agreed and said he had to visit the facilities so she could wait in her car for the police and him. She went to her car and he went around back.

The police car came as she got in her car and went directly to park in the special slip on the side of the building. The two officers got out and headed for the door from that side so Jo headed for the door from her parking place.

Just as the police came to the door it opened and Arlene stood there with a pistol in her hand. The officers were standing behind the door she had opened and she couldn't see them there. She pointed the pistol at Jo and snarled, "Let's see you win this one, you lousy goddamned bitch!"

A hand reached from behind the door and slapped the pistol downward just as Arlene pulled the trigger. The bullet ricocheted off the pavement two feet from her. The officer stepped around the door and slapped handcuffs onto Arlene's wrists in one smooth motion. "Ma'am, you are under arrest on a charge of attempted murder in the first degree!" he said.

Arlene swore long and colorfully.

"Call? We received no call," Sgt. Perkins said. "We stopped at the rest stop because we always stop there as we go on duty to see there has been no vandalism. Young punk thugs will paint all kinds of radical trash on the walls. Maybe Vic Owens, on the desk, took your call. Sometimes he can't get through on the radio when there's an electrical storm like this one.

"I can't seem to find any signs of this Tyana person. The key is still on the rack for the restroom inside the building.

"You said Watersham Under Makebridge? There are a few farms and a small mill on a creek there, I believe. We come from the main dispatch unit at Green Hills. There's only one officer at Watersham and he's there to keep the paperwork and take reports if he has to call anyone in.

"Truth be told, Ma'am, I've heard of this Merlin person before. Criminal analyst, but I think London. The Yard.

"Whatever, you might say out arrival was most timely."

"That is an understatement," Jo corrected.

### *But Then...*

Sylvia Nesmith sighed heavily and shook her head. *Here we go again!*

Jillie Ann, her sister, was in love. Again. For the umpteenth time. With a no-good motorcycle bum who needed a place to, as he called it, "crash" for awhile until his check came in. It was a disability compensation check he got every month since the accident.

What "The Accident" was, he never mentioned. By the look of him he would spend any check on booze or drugs – assuming he even got a check. There was no sign of any disability Syl could note. He was a big man who had no trouble climbing or lifting. He moved without apparent restriction.

He was a bum. Period. Probably a drug user and definitely someone who drank too much alcohol. He bragged about how much vodka he could swill and still handle that loud motorcycle. To call him a vulgar pig was being unkind to pigs.

Jillie always ended up with that kind. It was plainly merely personal stupidity. She was rebelling against her parents, who had died three years ago when their balcony on the fifth floor suddenly fell. Why it fell was not really known. It was steel and was bolted through the wall. They had been on the thing hundreds of times with no problem. The inspectors said something about a loose bolt or something – a cover-up for the contractor, Syl would bet! They probably forgot to put the bolts on in the first place or put them on so loosely that people walking around on the balcony would cause them to work loose.

## But Then...

Jillie didn't seem too upset by their deaths. She had always been a discipline problem to them and there was some resentment because they bought the condo and wouldn't allow Jillie to live alone until she could afford it. She had left for two weeks, then come back because she couldn't make enough money with her (rather bad) art. She was going to live with a man in his thirties, but she wasn't yet seventeen at the time and they said if she was even alone with him in some hotel room one time as a visitor he was going to be locked up for five years for contributing.

She had gone to stay with her Uncle Harry, but that lasted exactly twenty two hours. He was a bitter man who had always been jealous that his sister had married so well and that she had the two daughters. He tried to take his ire out on Jillie. He had been nasty to Syl when she came to pick Jillie up. He lived in a building on the next block that was old and slightly rundown. He seemed to hold even that against the girls.

He had visited sometimes when the parents were alive, but they didn't want him around. He was too negative and mean all the time. He was jealous of all of them and showed it.

Syl nor Jillie would have a thing to do with him if he wasn't their only close relative.

Since her parents died Jillie had a string of losers like this Arnold character. Syl had full control of the inheritance until Jillie was 21 years old. Two and a half more years. Syl didn't doubt she would go through the inheritance in a month. One of her great loves would take it and go.

She sighed again and said he could stay in the unused storeroom downstairs. He was not going to stay in the condo. Period.

Jillie slammed out and said Syl would pay for that! She

hated the sight of her!

She would come back later and say Syl had been right and there had to be something wrong with her that she couldn't see what a no-good sleazebag creep Arnold was. She loved Syl for protecting her from those bums that all men seemed to be and blah, blah, blah.

Jillie wanted to be independent and didn't know how. They were usually very close. This happened about twice a year. It would be nasty for the few days before Arnold did something that told her what he was.

Probably it would be like the last two times. Jillie would tell him she had money she was waiting for and leave the impression she could get part of it now. He would find she couldn't and would be gone.

She sighed once again and went to the kitchen, checked over the food at hand and headed for the super.

On the way home she was almost brained by a flowerpot that fell off a balcony on the third floor of the condo. That was the third time something like that had happened.

She had phenomenal luck, but it was a little scary. It was luck in both ways. The thing did drop almost on her, which was the bad luck, but missed her, which was the good.

She picked up the bag of groceries she had dropped and went to the elevator. That Arnold bum got off.

Wait! What was he doing upstairs? Surely Jillie wouldn't let him in the apartment! She wasn't about to cross Syl about that!

When she got to the apartment Jillie was in the shower. The CD player was on *Total Eclipse of the Heart*, the fourth song. Jillie always put it on when she went to the shower. She had been in there for about fifteen minutes. Arnold had not been there, but then, you can start any song you want by using the

*But Then...*

skip.

Syl felt a small premonition of fear. She wondered if maybe Arnold had been on the third floor. It would make sense. He would believe Jillie could get the money immediately if something happened to her. She was going to be very careful about where she went and who else was around. She was going to look up at the balconies before she walked under them from now on!

Jillie came out of the shower a few minutes later wrapping her hair in a towel. She said she was going to eat out, so don't bother to make up any of her vile recipes, then started to cry, then got a little defiant again. She said Arnold had said some awful things about her friends and maybe she should be careful about what else he said and did. Syl had been right before about people. Then she got defiant again and said some more nasty things.

Syl went into the kitchen and made a pot of coffee. Jillie would have a cup, she was sure. Maybe it was finally dawning on her that Syl was only trying to protect her.

Jillie was very quiet, drank about half a cup of coffee, said she had to think about some things and went out. She said to tell Arnold that she went to Cindy's house if he called. She needed to be away from him to think. Cindy was in France. No one would know where she was.

"Call me if you want to talk," Syl requested. Jillie got defiant, then said she couldn't think. She might call.

She left.

Syl made a potato and veggie pork pie. When Jillie got back there would be plenty. It was better if it had time to cool before you ate it.

Jillie called and asked Syl to meet her at Little Dog. She was reticent to go because it looked like it was about to rain

*But Then...*

cats and dogs, but agreed. It would be better to talk right there in the condo, but then....

The rain started just as she reached the place. Jillie ran in about three minutes after her. The place was packed, but there was one table off to the side that seated four and only had one man sitting there. Syl went to ask him if they could join him. She was a bit flustered. He was the most handsome man she had ever seen who wasn't on a TV or movie screen!

He smiled a perfect smile, removed the Homburg (she heard they were popular as rain hats now) and said he could use the company of such charming ladies. Syl could tell Jillie was as stricken by him as she was.

They chatted about various little things. He introduced himself as Merlin Tyana and said he was a situation analyst. Jillie asked what that was and he said he investigated things for the police, mostly. He tried to defuse tense or dangerous situations where people could be hurt.

"Some people make the same mistakes over and over. There is often something that makes the basis of the situation clear to someone who stands back far enough to see the whole picture. Too close and you only see bits and pieces. I have a talent to make people see why they do a thing, then they can face whatever pressures them to act in a negative way.

"Most self-destructive people have something that causes a bad reaction to things, usually authority. They know the authority is more concerned with protecting them than causing them grief, but react in the wrong fashion. The damage is done before they realize they were wrong.

"People tend to be too forgiving of things and to allow themselves to become doormats, which only encourages the abuser into even more damaging action. The abuser becomes

*But Then...*

rather expert at feigning remorse, thus causing the abused to find even more abuse shortly down that path.

"Sorry. My personal subject. I suppose you find it boring."

Syl tried to focus on his eyes that seemed to almost glow. He seemed somehow indistinct as a result. Jillie was doing about the same. She was trying to find something wrong with him, but there didn't seem to be anything at all. He was beautiful, strong, magnetic and had a perfectly modulated baritone voice. She would estimate he was twenty eight or nine years old.

She couldn't understand why she wanted to find something wrong with him. It was because Syl would say she should find someone like him. She couldn't argue that point!

"I'm one of the screwed up type," Jillie said. "Syl always says I'm self-destructive. I guess I am."

"Oh? Tell me about it?"

"Jillie's self-destructive and I'm the floormat, but I know she'll grow out of it."

"I don't know why I do the things I do," Jillie admitted. "I know Syl's right about my boyfriends, but that just makes me want them more to spite her."

"We're a spiteful family." She told Merl, as he insisted they call him, about the family, such as it was.

"Why did you go to your uncle when you knew how he would act?" Merl asked. "It would seem you would avoid him more than your sister because he was worse about such things."

"Well, he had introduced me to John, the one the fight was about. We met right here in the Little Dog by accident and John was there and knew him and asked that Uncle Harry introduce us. I thought he would understand, but he said I was acting like a little whore and I should face the fact that

I'd never be anything else.

"He's a terrible person. I just didn't feel there was anyplace else to go."

"Harry has never introduced me to anyone who I'd care to be seen with," Syl said. "I find him to be a little bit scary. He says things that seem totally devoid of caring about anyone or anything other than himself. I thought of going to him because of the almost accidents, but know it would be a waste of time."

Merl insisted she tell him about the almost accidents. She did.

"Hmm. It would seem this Arnold character could well be behind one of the incidents. Was he around for any of the others?"

"No. Just this one. John was around for the first one. Ken was around for the next."

"There's no one who was around for all of them except ..." Syl began. She was looking at Jillie strangely.

"No," Merl said quickly. "Jillie isn't the type."

"Then they were accidents," Syl said tiredly. "There was no one else."

"Oh, there was always one other. Right down the block."

"Harry? I can't ... why? Because he's the only relative and would inherit everything!"

"Oh, god!" Jillie cried. "What do we do?"

"See that he gets nothing if anything happens to either or both of you," Merl said sternly. "Make wills that leave it all to medical research except for one pound to him."

"But ... he killed our folks?" Syl asked.

"It's altogether possible," Merl replied. "It may be impossible to prove, but you can protect yourselves and each other. I suspect he's been directing these bums to you so it can be claimed one of them was responsible when something happens to you, Jillie. He planted the rebellion in you and has been using it."

"I see. We can thwart him trying to kill us off. We can handle that as soon as the rain stops. Our lawyer is in the building right across the street and can make the wills for us," Syl suggested. "Thank you, Merl. You may have saved our lives."

"Speaking of the rain, I see it is much less. I must be on my way. It has been most pleasant." Merl stood, put on his Homburg, smiled, nodded and went toward the door. Some people passed between and he never seemed to reach the door.

Strange.

Syl and Jillie finished their coffee and went across the street to the office of their barrister. The will was drawn up and certified before they left his office to head home.

Uncle Harry would be notified that the will was made and that he got one pound as reward for being an obnoxious ass to them for years.

## _Smoke_

"... isn't always true. There is often smoke with no fire," Sir Dennis concluded.

"Balderdash!" Lord Chinton replied. "We are speaking of an expression, not a scientific study!

"The expression was used because of repeated accusations by so many uninvolved persons. I should have said that there is far too much evidence, though anecdotal, that something rather sinister is going on with that individual.

"What do you say, Sir ... Merlin, was it?"

"Just Merl. I'm one of those who think titles are rather silly," Merlin Tyana replied. "I'm must plead I have no knowledge of the basis of this conversation. I only arrived a moment ago and was seated here through some former arrangement. I admit to being a stranger to this place and these proceedings. I was invited because I am an analyst and my sponsor believes I may offer some insight from another angle of view, if you will. Had the storm outside struck earlier I would probably not be here as I am, in this situation, an interloper.

"This is to be a study of evidential process. I must assume that you are speaking of some case in the past, or one in the present?"

"A small bit of both," Sir Reginald answered. "Perhaps we may tender our evidence in a more chronological order. An analyst sounds like someone who peruses the evidence and reaches a conclusion?"

"Yes – or tries to find some conclusive mot. I would appreciate a quick outline in chronological order. It is not impossible I might clear away some of the smoke.

*Smoke*

"How close are you to the problem? Perhaps it would vest well to step back to where the entire picture is in view. When we stand too close we too often miss details."

"Eh, yes," Sir Dennis said. "The problem is something that started, apparently, on the order of ten years ago when a popular lass, Sharon Chesterton, disappeared. As it was during or after a visit to this very hall, it became a topic of discussion. We were each involved, then or later.

"There was a Grand Debutante Ball for the girl. She was sixteen years of age that day and her parents – fine people, I must say – presented her to society.

"She was most popular, a true lady in the finest senses of the word. She was more than average attractive, both in personality and appearance. She was certainly the Belle of the Ball then, if I may be trite of expression.

"Be that as it may, she was last seen saying her good nights at that entranceway just beyond the vestibule where you entered. She was speaking with her father and mother, somewhat heatedly, by account of various persons, myself among them, thence took herself out and into the parking lot.

"She has not again been seen unto this day by anyone who can say with definite knowledge that it was, indeed Sharon Chesterton that they saw. She has supposedly been seen in both London and Liverpool and into Hartfordshire and to the north.

"There exists, it would seem, no evidence to point toward any specific direction. Whether she is alive and well and hiding from her former friends and acquaintances or laying buried in some makeshift grave somewhere is the question.

"The reference to smoke was concerning the fact that those people of good character have insisted they have seen her. Often. That is the too much smoke that presupposes a fire."

*Smoke*

"I suspect you have left out as much as you have told me," Merl replied. "What was the argument with her parents in reference of? Under what circumstances was she seen? Who was the boyfriend the argument was about is, perhaps, more to the point."

"Boyfriend? I have heard nothing about any boyfriend!" Lord Chinton exclaimed.

"It is an obvious assumption to aid analysis," Merl replied. "A young girl, the debutante ball, an argument with the parents, a disappearance, persons seeing her at various times in various places – how would you add those facts?"

"The argument concerned the loss of some jewelry that Miss Chesterton was wearing. There was no boyfriend." Sir Dennis replied. "We have, of course, had alerts out from that time concerning the location of the jewelry since that very night. No items of their description or value have appeared anywhere.

"That bunch who were fencing and recutting jewels who were caught just a week later were probably the thieves."

"Hmm. So the jewelry disappeared, the girl disappeared, but has supposedly been seen – and there is no boyfriend? That escapes logic.

"Has anyone who saw the girl spoken to her? Was she close enough that there was no question of her identity?"

"Er, of course. She is a very distinctive person. Her pride is of the same order as her mother. Her hair is a most unusual color. A golden red with shadings that are not so easy to describe. She wears it long. She has an outstanding figure and is quite tall," Sir Reginald explained. "I was one who saw her. In London, it was. She was entering the hotel where I had gained lodging as I went out the other portal. We were no more than eight feet apart. I called to her, but she went inside. I went around and sought her in the lobby, but she was not there. The personnel in the hotel did not recognize the description and the police never found anywhere else she might have stayed.

"Cowel Donlevy saw her in the north. She was in a small restaurant at a table about twenty feet away. She was speaking with a somewhat unsavory type, seeming to have taken offense at something. Cowel moved toward them, but was stopped by a divider wall. She had made her exit while he went around to the divide access. He knew her from working for her parents until a few weeks before the ball. He was let go as a savings measure. The economy was quite in the doldrums ten years ago, you will remember.

"He said it could not have been anyone else. The hair and figure are that distinctive. She had aged six years when he saw her, but was still as beautiful and was, he swears, Sharon Chesterton or her twin.

"The information was given to the police, but they could find no track of her."

"I see. And her parents efforts to locate her? What was the direction of that?"

"Er, she was always a bit headstrong. They were not worried for the first two or three days, believing she would return, contrite, as she had done in the past," Lord Chinton answered. "They became quite alarmed when she didn't return."

"I see. And the missing jewelry? It was never recovered?"

"No. After six months the insurance paid off. The jewels have never reappeared," Sir Dennis replied.

"The stones were large enough to have been cut?"

"Er, yes. That is probably what happened," Sir Reginald said.

"Yes. Before the ball," Merlin said dryly. "Has Sharon or her body been sought here?"

"Here?"

"On the estate of her parents. In the immediate surrounding area."

"Well! Most certainly! Immediately after her disappearance they looked almost everywhere," Lord Chinton exclaimed. "What, Sir, are you suggesting? Not, I sincerely hope, what it sounds like?"

"I am suggesting nothing. I am analyzing a situation.

"Only the mother could be posing as Sharon with any hope of success. The jewelry brought the parents out of debt, there was...."

"How dare you, Sir! They were not in debt at the time! George sold some land in the north for a substantial profit a month before the ball and was entirely out of debt! He would have much preferred the jewelry for his wife than the fifty thousand pounds from the insurance! How dare you!" Lord Chinton exploded.

"I tend to agree, but must give credit to the fact no one told Sir Merlin about any land sale nor any lack of debt. I can well understand, since we tendered evidence in that Cowel was let go of service for financial reasons, that an incorrect idea was formed," Sir Dennis said calmly. "As Sir Merlin voiced at the beginning, one must see all the details to form a coherent picture. I apologize for placing Sir Merlin into a position where such a sad conclusion must logically be assumed."

"Er, well, yes," Lord Chinton said, a bit suspiciously.

"Perhaps, but nothing has changed," Merlin said. "Only the mother could be posing as her daughter. It is very obvious that such is the case. The only reasonable path is to ask why.

*Smoke*

The jewelry being taken at that time and situation makes some things more than obvious.

"Before the indignation, consider what a person trying to hide would do that was definitely not done. To what purpose was it not done?"

"I *am* indignant! What, Sir, are you trying to do here? I demand explanation!" Lord Chinton cried.

"A moment here. I think I see what Sir Merlin is saying. He could hardly come to any other conclusion, under the circumstances," Sir Reginald said. "The hair."

"Hair? What the hell?" Lord Chinton yelled so that people at adjoining tables turned.

"The hair," Sir Reginald said. "If you have a feature so distinctive that it would identify you and you did not wish to be found, what do you do?

"If it is a hair length and color, you cut and dye the hair. To do otherwise will most certainly draw attention to you – exactly that which you supposedly wish to avoid.

"Why no one in the area remembered seeing her before or after the encounters would tend to make one wonder if such a person was actually in any of those places. The police looked for her or a woman of her description in all cases, yet never found anyone else who had remarked her.

"I think it is well that we investigate that land sale."

"But! You are suggesting that ... I will not countenance this!" Lord Chinton threw down his serviette and stalked away from the table. The others seemed a bit embarrassed. Sir Dennis said to look at the situation from the angle presented to Sir Merlin left only one conclusion to be reached as to what the sightings were about. The fact remained that Sharon was the daughter and had disappeared. Why?

"I think the problem will prove to be that the jewels Sharon was wearing were fakes. The parents sold the jewels earlier to gain the capital to continue. The jewels were stolen there and it would come out quite soon, should the thief try to have them appraised, that they were false," Merlin explained. "Something happened ... I am having trouble with that one thing. It is the one single way it could be, but how Sharon discovered the jewels were false needs explanation."

"She certainly could not have learned of any such thing that very night," Sir Reginald said, thinking. "I have met, even know, her parents. I have always wondered why they seemed to be so unconcerned for so long.

"What if she did go home the next day or so and discovered that her parents had done such a deal to relieve their financial situation? What would they do?

"I don't picture them harming her. That is where I make no sense of it."

"I think they would not intentionally harm the girl," Merlin agreed. "However, please note the 'intentional' part. It should be easy to resolve. That land sale will answer many questions and this Cowel person holds, I am almost certain, a very important piece of the puzzle."

"There, I fail ... so! Why was Cowel let go? The financial situation was resolved before that event!" Sir Reginald cried. "Why, then, was he removed from employment? Could it be because he was aware there was no land sale? Could he know something about those jewels that he isn't aware he knows?

"He would never stoop to extortion. If he knew he had the information he would tender it.

"One more little detail we have not considered about Cowel. He is from the area where the land was supposedly sold."

"Well, I must take my leave," Merlin said. "I have another

appointment and the storm is subsiding. I wish all of you well. I hope you can resolve this. That girl and her memory must not be tarnished by what was not her doing, has she not done anything.

"Elsewise, it should be known if she did do anything, though I rather doubt that is the case. I believe what may have happened was as much as accidental. I believe what led up to it was as certainly not." He nodded and left as Lord Chinton returned, looking sheepish.

"Where is Sir Merlin off to?" he asked. "I must apologize for my actions. I have checked with Cowel by telephone. He tells me that he was never aware that the Chestertons held any land in his vicinity. Sir Merlin was correct in that assessment and I reacted very badly and without due consideration."

"But you had to pass him!" Sir Reginald cried. "He left not half a minute ago! He would have to have been in the vestibule when you came through!"

"I saw no one," Lord Chinton replied. "I have alerted Lieutenant Chambers, the head officer in the case, of that fact. He has been investigating Sharon's disappearance from the first and has become somewhat obsessed with finding a solution. I have also wondered about things is why I reacted so strongly. I was hearing what I suspected while pretending to myself that I had no such suspicions. Guilt complex, you see.

"Well, we shall see what we shall see, what? Chambers will communicate with Cowel and will face the Chestertons with what is learned. He will report on the morrow.

"Smithers! Did Sir Merlin Tyana check out or is he still on the premises?"

The man who all members and guests had to pass entering

## *Smoke*

or exiting, Smithers, came to ask who he was talking about. The was no Sir Merlin Tyana in attendance.

They explained he came as a guest of someone and had sat right there, talking with them He left not five minutes past.

"No one of that name has entered or left," Smithers said stiffly. "I would have noted them and made them sign the register."

Sir Reginald laughed. "Now we have a REAL mystery! The one we discussed was smoke and mirrors. Is this one all smoke or all mirror?"

Two nights later they were all at the same table. Lieutenant Chambers was there to report on the arrest of the Chestertons for fraud. They had sold the jewels and had paste copies made that they produced for such as the ball. They were stolen and the fear was that they would be declared false.

"That would have meant nothing or less. They were the property of the Chestertons and the Chestertons had the right to do with them as they pleased. They did not have the right to file for insurance, but saw that as a way to escape the debt they were accumulating when they were stolen.

"I asked what had happened to their daughter. The mother said she had disappeared, as we were aware. The father was silent. I asked her to please explain her posing as her daughter, if that were the case. Why did she want it to appear the daughter was alive and well?

"I said we had witnesses as to the fact that was what she had done. She refused to speak further without her barrister present.

"We are exploring that estate. I, personally, feel we will discover the daughter's body there somewhere. As you each know the estate, where is the likely place?"

*Smoke*

Sir Reginald looked thoughtful. He said the logical place, considering the family, was in the cemetery on the property. He couldn't believe there was deliberate murder involved. They would want a decent grave for her.

Chambers made a call and sat to talk about the case awhile. He received a call half an hour later. There was a very suspicious displacement of a casket in the mausoleum.

A few minutes later he got a call that her body was in the casket. It had been put in an unfilled niche in the wall. The father was confronted and explained that she had come home late and accused him of fraud. Her boyfriend had taken the jewels so they could have the funds to run away together. He discovered very quickly that the jewels were paste copies. She wanted to know just what was going on.

The father had reacted in fury that she had been seeing this person behind their backs and had slapped her. She slapped him back and he pushed her. She was at the top of the stairs and had fallen down. Her neck was broken. She was dead. He and his wife took her body to the mausoleum and placed her in a casket and sealed it in an unused niche. The whole mystery was solved, at last.

"Except for the real mystery," Sir Reginald said. "*Who* – and, perhaps more to the point, *what* – is Sir Merlin Tyana?"

C. D. Moulton's works are available on most major outlets as printed or e-books. CD writes the CD Grimes, PI mysteries, the Det. Lt. Nick Storie mysteries, the Clint Faraday mysteries, the Flight of the Maita science fiction series, books on orchid culture and many others of many types. Mystery, adventure, intrigue, science fiction, fantasy, paranormal, mild erotica, and factual.

CPSIA information can be obtained
at www.ICGtesting.com
Printed in the USA
BVHW030304060922
646255BV00015B/498